Accelerated Reader

B.L. _____

Points _____

Do not Dread Wetting the Bed

by Paul M. Kramer

Do not Dread Wetting the Bed by Paul M. Kramer

© Paul M. Kramer November 2011. All Rights Reserved.

Aloha Publishers LLC
333 Dairy Road, Suite 106
Kahului, HI 96732
www.alohapublishers.com

Inquiries, comments or further information are available at, www. alohapublishers.com.

Illustrations by BJ Nartker, bjnartker@comcast.net.

ISBN 13 (EAN): 978-0-9819745-0-7
Library of Congress Control Number (LCCN): 2009902664
Printed in China

Do not Dread Wetting the Bed
by Paul M. Kramer

This book is dedicated to all kids who have wet their beds.

Do not Dread Wetting the Bed

by Paul M. Kramer

PUBLISHERS
Books & Stories by Paul M. Kramer

This is a story about you and Cynthia Claire.
Cynthia is five years old and lives in Delaware.
We want to help both of you because we really care.
Bedwetting is a problem for kids who live everywhere.

Waking up soaked often makes Cynthia cry.
Sometimes Cynthia's parents do not understand why.
She tells them I am sorry, much harder I will try.
I will try, very, very hard, to wake up dry.

Some habits are good and some habits are bad.
Bed wetting is a problem that so many people have had.
Waking up in the middle of the night can make anyone sad.
Has bed wetting ever happened to either your mom or your dad?

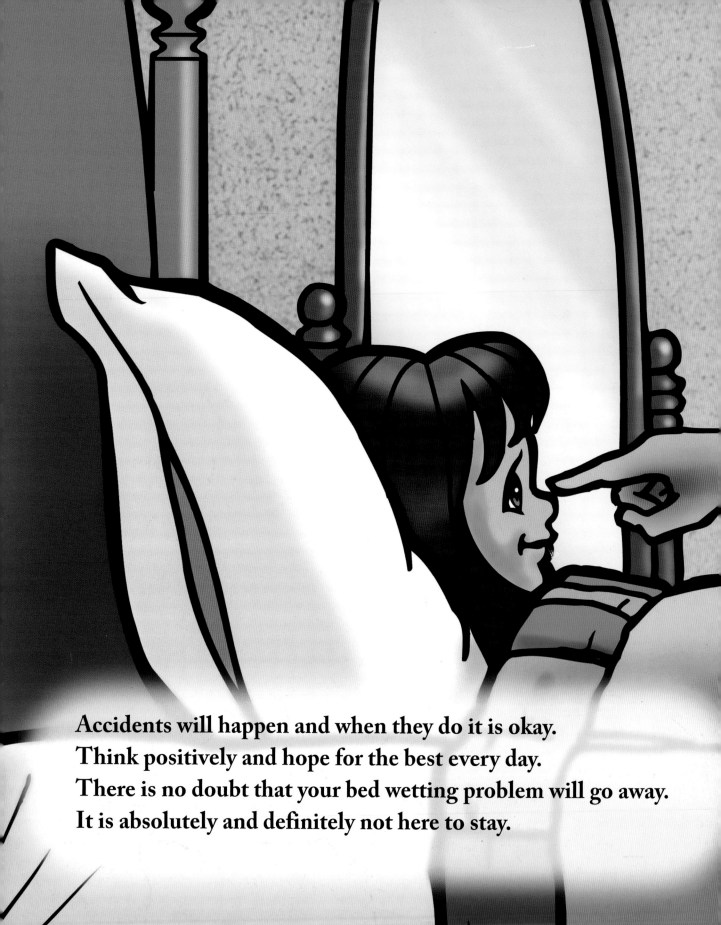

Accidents will happen and when they do it is okay.
Think positively and hope for the best every day.
There is no doubt that your bed wetting problem will go away.
It is absolutely and definitely not here to stay.

Anyone who wets their bed dreads the thought of bed wetting.
It can certainly be depressing and quite upsetting.
Just ask Jed or Ed or Winifred.
Unfortunately they all still wet their bed.

Sometimes while you are sleeping you feel the need to go.
Before you realize what is happening to you it begins to flow.
That warm wet feeling that you have unfortunately come to know.
You, your cover, your sheets, are all soaked, oh no, oh no.

Please use the toilet immediately before you go to sleep.
You will be more likely to sleep until the morning without a peep.
Do not drink liquids before you go to bed.
The next morning you may just wake up dry instead.

Bedwetting affects children regardless if they are rich or poor.
Unfortunately, with bedwetting there is no simple or easy cure.
It's time for the pee-pee monsters to leave and walk out the door.
Pee-pee monsters are no longer welcome to live here anymore.

Having a bedwetting problem can cause a bed wetter lots of stress.
Don't be too hard on yourself after you've made a mess.
It's easy to see why someone could get depressed.
But I promise you that as time goes on, it will happen less and less.

Your bladder is still small and so are you.
Bedwetting is an embarrassing problem to have to go through.
Can you think of anything else that we could do,
to help stop the wetting of your bed from happening
to Cynthia and you?

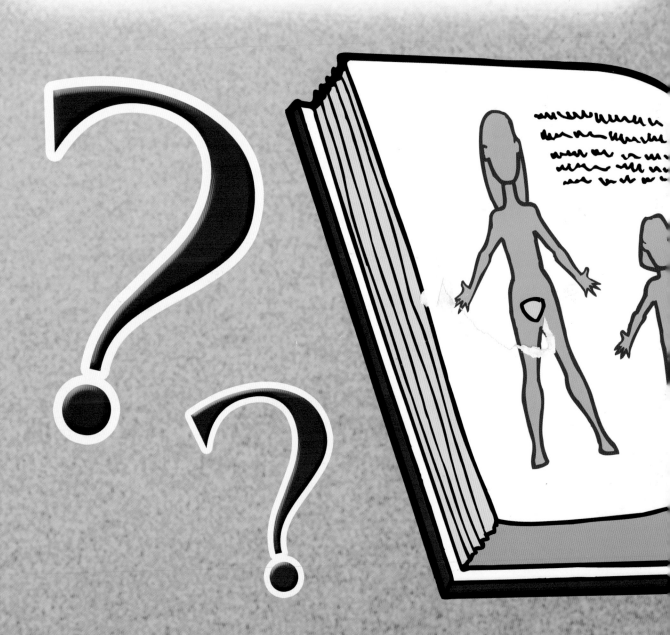

KIDS WET THEIR BEDS

Some habits are good and some habits are bad.
Bed wetting is a problem that people all around the world have had.
Changing the bedding in the middle of the night can make anyone really sad.
Ask if the same bed wetting problem happened to your mom or your dad.

If you have an accident here or there, it is really quite okay.
Think positively and hope for the best each and every day.
There is no doubt that your bed wetting will eventually go away.
It is absolutely and definitely not here to stay.

Please use the toilet immediately before you go to sleep.
You might sleep until the morning without a peep.
Also do not drink liquids right before bed.
The next morning you may just wake up dry instead.

Your bladder is still small and so are you.
Bedwetting is an embarrassing problem to have to go through.

Paul M Kramer

Just Published by Paul M. Kramer

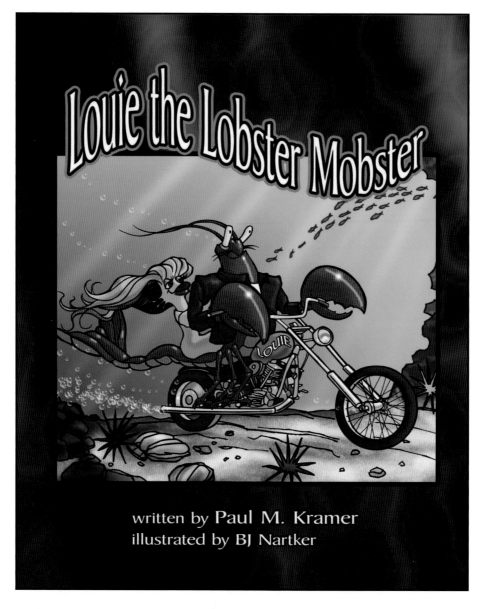

Is there anyone in this underworld community who can stand up to Louie and his mob? This is a clever story about good versus evil. A dapper wealthy lobster and his sea creature mobster crew shake down hard-working businesses that are trying to make a living. Good eventually triumphs over evil and crime ultimately does not pay. The hero's here are the business owners and the forces of good. Alone, they are vulnerable and easily bullied but together they are strong, and ultimately prevail.

ISBN 13 (EAN): 978-0-9819745-2-1
Size: 8 inches by 10 inches
Retail Price: $15.95

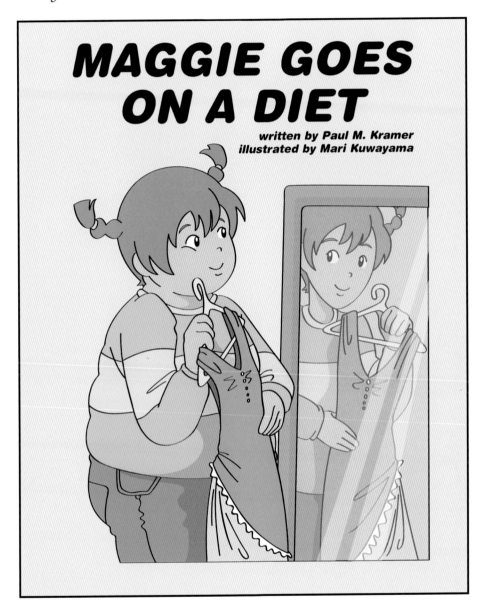

This book is about a 14 year old girl who changed her eating habits and began playing sports. She started eating and enjoying healthy and nutritious foods which slowly began to transform her life. Maggie became happier and more physically fit. Through time, exercise and hard work, Maggie's self image and confidence improved steadily.

ISBN 13 (EAN): 978-0-9819745-5-2
Size: 8 inches by 10 inches
Retail Price: $15.95

About the Author

Paul M Kramer lives in Hawaii on the Island of Maui, but was born and raised in New York City. He moved to the Rainbow and Aloha State of Hawaii in 1995 with his wife Cindy and their then infant son, Lukas. After being in Hawaii for about nine years, Mr. Kramer's true passion in life was awakened. He began writing children's books that deal with important issues that kids face today. Mr. Kramer's books are written in rhyme, are easy to read and make learning fun.